The ^very^ Fairy Princess
TEACHER'S PET

by Julie Andrews *&* Emma Walton Hamilton

Illustrated by Christine Davenier

LITTLE, BROWN & COMPANY
LB kids

Hi! My name is Gerry.

I am a fairy princess!

I know because I feel it in my heart.

A fairy princess is kind and loving.

She is a friend to all, big and small.

Great news!

Next week is spring vacation.

LOTS of time to play.

(Even a fairy princess needs some time off!)

Miss Pym asks who can look after Houdini,
our class pet.

She says it must be someone very caring.

Who is more caring than a fairy princess?

I bring Houdini home.
I am going to give him
the most SPARKLY week of his life!
He will meet all my family,
and we will play and play.
(Fairy princesses always show
a friend a good time!)

The first day, I do not see Houdini.

He hides in his bed all day.

I think he must be scared to be someplace new.

I sing to him to help
him feel more at home.
He does not come out.

I paint him a picture of our classroom.
He still does not come out.

I try ALL my best tricks, but nothing works.

At bedtime, I am almost asleep
when I hear a noise.
SQUEAK! SQUEAK! SQUEAK!
I turn on the light.

Houdini is running on his wheel.
I tell him I am happy to see him,
but it is time for bed.
He does not listen.

I read him a bedtime story.

He still does not listen.

I try all my best tricks to get him to sleep.

Nothing works.

I am awake ALL night.

The next day, I have to clean his cage.
It smells funny, so I hold my breath.
(A fairy princess gets a job done
even if it is yucky.)

Then Houdini runs out of his cage!

I race after him, but it is too late.

He zooms right out of my room!

Everyone helps me look for him.

Daddy looks under the sofa.

Mommy looks in the kitchen.

My brother, Stewart, looks in his trumpet.
No Houdini.

Where could he be?

What if I never find him?

How will I explain to Miss Pym?

This is the most UN-sparkly week of my life!

But a fairy princess never loses hope.

It is time to put on my thinking crown!

Mommy gives me milk and cookies
to help me think.
YUM! I eat every bite.
Then I get a great idea!

I remember the snacks Houdini likes.

He likes nuts, seeds, grapes, and dog biscuits.

I make snack trails ALL over the house.

Each one leads to his cage.

24

Mommy hates a messy house.

I tell her a missing friend

is more important than a clean house.

(Fairy princesses are VERY loyal.)

After dinner, I check the cage.

No Houdini.

But the dog biscuits are missing from the trail!

I fill in the gaps with extra nuts.

At bedtime, I try to keep my eyes open.
It is too hard.

I nod, nod, nod.

SQUEAK! SQUEAK! SQUEAK!

Houdini is running on his wheel!

His cheeks are STUFFED with snacks!

I am SO glad to see him!

I close the door to his cage.

I tell him he can squeak as MUCH as he wants.

I just want him to be happy.

Even a fairy princess must remember
to let friends sparkle
in their OWN special way!

The ^very Fairy Princess

Punch-out Activity!

Houdini has escaped!
Spin the disk to get him
back in his cage.

Instructions:

- Punch out the large circle along the perforations.
- Punch out both small circles and discard.
- Gather two rubber bands and ask an adult to help you cut each one to make two straight lines.
- Tie one rubber band to each hole with a double knot.
- Wind up the disk by holding one string in each hand and twirling the disk ten times without letting go.

OR

Ask someone to hold the ends of each rubber band, pulling the disk tight. Spin the disk around ten times without letting go.

When you release the disk, Houdini will magically appear in his cage!